Sir Alexander Mackenzie School
61 Sir Winston Churchill Ave.
St. Albert AB
T8N 0G5

THE DAY OCEAN CAME TO VISIT

THE DAY OCEAN CAME TO VISIT

by Diane Wolkstein

paintings by Steve Johnson *and* Lou Fancher

Gulliver Books   Harcourt, Inc.

San Diego   New York   London

Printed in Singapore

Long ago, Sun and Moon lived on earth. They lived in a large house that Sun had built from long bamboo poles. He made their roof very high, because both he and Moon were very tall.

Sun liked to travel. Every day he set out in a different direction to explore the world. Moon preferred to stay home, working in her garden. She grew all kinds of flowers and vegetables, and made beautiful curving paths leading from one part of her garden to another. Every evening Sun and Moon ate dinner and sat on their porch, chatting happily together.

One morning Sun rode farther than he had ever gone. At the edge of the earth he met a woman named Ocean. Ocean was lively, friendly, and very talkative. She talked about ships and storms and pirates and treasures.

She talked and talked, until finally she stopped and said, "Excuse me, I hope I'm not talking too much."

"Please go on," Sun assured her. "I've never met anyone who has had such exciting adventures."

After another hour, Ocean paused and said, "Excuse me, please tell me if I'm talking too much."

"No, no. Your stories are wonderful. As soon as I get home, I will tell them to my wife, Moon, who also loves stories."

"I'd like to meet your wife," Ocean said. "I've heard she is very beautiful. Please invite her to visit."

Moon enjoyed hearing about Ocean's exciting life, so Sun said, "Ocean has invited you to visit. Why don't you come with me to hear more stories?"

But Moon answered, "I am happy working in my garden. You go and visit Ocean."

Ocean was delighted to see Sun again and began to talk at once. She talked about tropical islands and lavender sunsets and fiery volcanoes. Sun was amazed. Just a few days had passed and Ocean had had so many adventures. That night Sun again asked Moon to visit Ocean. But Moon said, "Let's invite Ocean to visit us. We can prepare a good meal for her, and she can see our garden."

The next day, as soon as Sun arrived, Ocean started to talk, but Sun interrupted, "Ocean! Moon and I would like to invite you to visit us."

"Oh, how nice," Ocean said. "Thank you, but I'm afraid I'd be too much for you."

"Why is that?" asked Sun.

"Well, there's a lot of me— shells and starfish and jellyfish and turtles and—"

"My house is large," Sun said.

"That's not all—there are dolphins and sea lions and walruses and sharks—"

"'Sharks'?" echoed Sun. "I ... I will make my house a little larger."

"—and mermaids and seaweed and crabs and mussels and whales."

"'Whales'? I ... I ... I will make my house very large!" Sun exclaimed.

That evening Sun told Moon, "Ocean has accepted our invitation. At first she was unwilling because she said she is too big. But I assured her that I would make our house a little larger."

"How big is Ocean?" asked Moon.

"Big," Sun answered.

So Sun went into the bamboo forest and cut down bamboo poles. He made their house twice as large.

"How big did you say Ocean is?"
Moon asked Sun.

"Very big," he answered. "I think I
will make our house a little larger." Sun
kept building, and soon their house
stretched nearly as far as the eye could
see.

At last they were ready for their guest. A fine dinner of yams, cassavas, and plantains was set on the table. Sun and Moon sat on the porch and waited. Suddenly Moon's nose twitched. "I smell something," she said. "A salty, briny smell."

"That's Ocean," Sun said. "She must be on her way."

Then Moon's ears moved. "I hear something," she said. "A low, deep rumbling."

"That's Ocean," Sun said eagerly. "She's getting closer."

Sun and Moon saw water spreading across the plains in the distance. Ocean was coming closer and closer. In a short time, Ocean arrived at their steps.

"Welcome!" Sun and Moon said happily.

"I hope I won't be too much trouble," Ocean said.

"Oh no, no," Sun reassured her.

Ocean came up the stairs and started to flow into the rooms. "I'm so glad to meet you," Ocean said to Moon.

"This way." Moon pointed, trying to lead Ocean into the dining room. But Ocean flowed into all the rooms. Ocean was talking, but they could not hear what she was saying. Ocean was everywhere. Sun and Moon felt something biting. Turtles and fish and seals and dolphins were swimming about inside their house. The water was rising, and still Ocean was flowing into their house. Moon looked out the window. She saw that her garden was covered with water!

Sun and Moon began to swim. They swam out the window of their house. They climbed up onto their roof. Water was in every direction. Sun, who was never afraid of anything, began to tremble. He said to Moon, "Where shall we go? What shall we do?"

Moon could see seals and mermaids and even a whale heading toward them. Suddenly she knew what to do. "Jump!" she cried.

They jumped.

Up, up, up, up, up, up, up they leaped, until they reached the top of the sky.

And that is where they are today, in the heavens. And that is where Moon gave birth to their little children—the stars.

Blessings on Phylis and Philip Morrison, whose presence and whose recounting of the tales of Moon's children inspires and delights all who know them
—D. W.

For William and Doris, who live by the sea
—S. J. & L. F.

Author's Acknowledgments

Thanks to those who graciously hosted Ocean: Jinx and Frank Roosevelt, Billie and Al Ballou, Marie-Monique and Ray Steckel, Susan Thomas and Peter Sills, Doreen Rappaport, Elizabeth Borsodi and Gary Wolkstein, and Francine Zucker.

This story is an adaptation of the creation myth "Why the Sun and Moon Live in the Sky" from Elphinstone Dayrell's collection, *Folk Stories from South Nigeria, West Africa* (1910).

Library of Congress Cataloging-in-Publication Data
Wolkstein, Diane.
The day Ocean came to visit/written by Diane Wolkstein; illustrated by Steve Johnson and Lou Fancher.
p. cm.
"Gulliver Books."
Summary: After hearing Ocean's stories, Sun invites Ocean to the house he shares with his wife, Moon, but his visitor proves to be more than his house can hold.
[1. Folklore—Nigeria.]   I. Johnson, Steve, 1960– ill.   II. Fancher, Lou, ill.   III. Title.
PZ8.1.W84Day   2001
398.8'09669'06—dc21   00-10898
ISBN 0-15-201774-7

First edition
H G F E D C B A

The illustrations in this book were done in oil on paper and shells on clay.
The display type was set in Sanvito.
The text type was set in Cochin.
Color separations by Bright Arts Ltd., Hong Kong
Printed and bound by Tien Wah Press, Singapore
This book was printed on totally chlorine-free Nymolla Matte Art paper.
Production supervision by Sandra Grebenar and Pascha Gerlinger
Designed by Lou Fancher